WILL YOU CARRY ME?

EDNA WALKER CHANDLER

Pictures by Meyer Seltzer

Albert Whitman & Company · Chicago

WILL YOU CARRY ME?

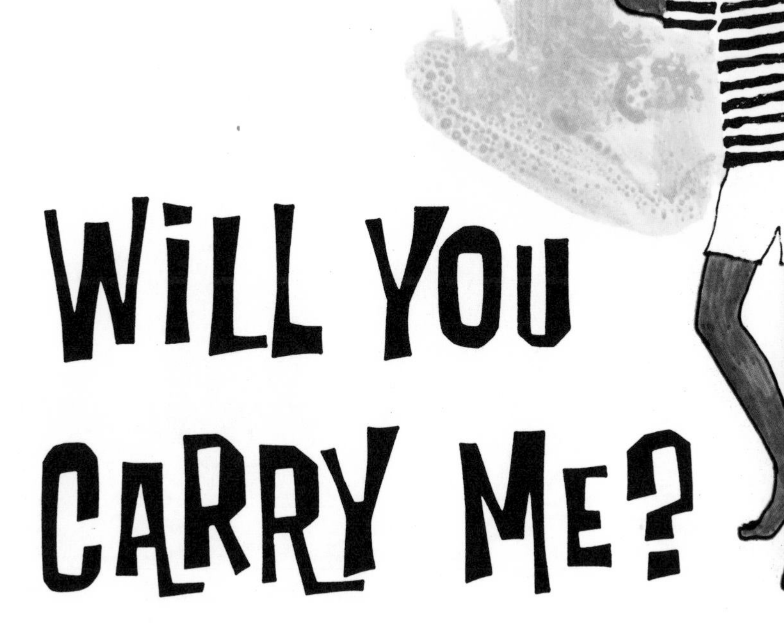

 L.C. Catalog Card 65-23881.
Published simultaneously in Canada by George J. McLeod, Ltd., Toronto.
Printed in U.S.A.

Gemo is an African boy. He lives in the small country of Liberia, which is about as big as the state of Tennessee. There are about as many people in Liberia as there are in Arizona.

Gemo knows that his country is more than one hundred years old. Like the United States, Liberia has a President. But in Liberia, only Negroes can be citizens.

Rain and hot weather—that's what Gemo sees a lot of from May until October. The very hottest month of the year is January.

Gemo speaks English, but it is a little different from the English you speak.

Mrs. Chandler, who wrote Gemo's story, lived in Liberia for two years. She went there to help Liberian teachers make books for their schools. So perhaps boys like Gemo are reading some of Mrs. Chandler's stories, just as you are when you turn the page.

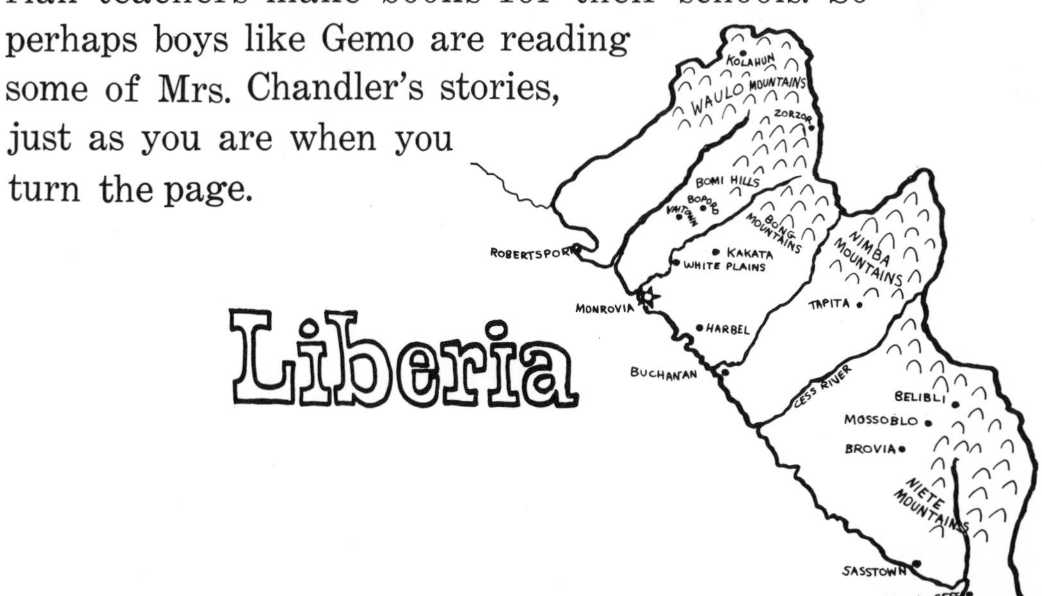

GEMO

had a big pan.
It was full of coconuts.
He put it on his head.

"This pan is heavy," Gemo said.
"It is too heavy."

He took two coconuts out.
“No, no!” said his mother.
“You must carry all the coconuts
to market.
We want money to buy fish.
We want plenty, plenty fish.”

Gemo put the two coconuts in the pan.
Now the pan was heavy again.
But he must carry all the coconuts
to market—his mother said so.
"You are big," she said.
"You can carry a big pan of coconuts."

His mother was right, Gemo was
a big boy.
The pan of coconuts was not
too heavy for him.

But Gemo was lazy.
He did not like to carry big loads.
How could he get the coconuts
to market without so much work?

All at once he thought of a way.
Gemo saw his big friend John
coming in the jeep.
"Hal-oo! Hal-oo, John! Stop!
Please stop!"

John made the jeep go slow.
Gemo came over to it.
"Will you carry me to market?"
he asked.
"The coconuts are heavy.
Please carry me."

"I can not carry you," John answered.
"This is not my jeep.
You know that.
I drive for Big Man who works
on the roads.
I can not carry you."

John sat tall and proud
in the driver's seat.

"OK, I go now," Gemo said,
and he stepped away from the jeep.

Gemo walked a little way.
A taxi came along and stopped.
Some people got out of the taxi.

Gemo hurried to the taxi and asked,
"Please, will you carry me?
My load is heavy.
It hurts my head.
Will you carry me to market?"

"Where is your money?" said the man.
"I will carry you if you have the money."

"I have no money," Gemo said in a small,
small voice.
The taxi went away.

Gemo walked on.
The sun climbed up, up in the sky.
The smell of good wet bush
made Gemo tired.
If only he could find someone to carry him!

Just then he saw a big cotton tree.
"Here is a big, big tree," he said.
"I will stop and rest."
Gemo put the pan of coconuts
on the ground.

The rice birds flew here and there
high in the ragged palm trees.
They made plenty, plenty palaver.
Talk, talk, talk!
"Lazy boy! Lazy boy!"

Gemo didn't even answer.
Silly birds!
What did they know about a big pan
of coconuts?

Gemo sat down beside his pan of coconuts.
Soon his head began to nod.
Suddenly he heard something.
He sat up quickly and rubbed his eyes
to see better.

A money bus!
"Aha!" he said. "I will give the bus man
a coconut, then he will carry me."

The money bus stopped.
Two people got out.
Three people ran to get in.
One had a heavy load that he tied
on the top of the bus.

"Will you carry me?" Gemo asked.
"Here is a fine coconut.
It is plenty, plenty fine-o."

The driver laughed.
"I have too many coconuts now," he said.
"Where do you want to go?"

"I want to go to market," Gemo said,
"and my pan is too heavy."

The bus man said, "That will cost ten cents.
Give me ten cents and I will carry you."

Gemo shook his head sadly.
"I only have coconuts," he said.
"A pan of big, heavy coconuts."

"That is too bad," said the driver.
"I go now."
He drove away.

Now the sun was high over Gemo's head.
He should be on the way home.
But he hadn't even gone to market yet!
Gemo put the pan of coconuts
back on his head.
He walked on and on.

An old man with a wheelbarrow came
from a little side path.
“Old Man,” Gemo said. “Please, Old Man,
will you carry me?”

Old Man stopped pushing the wheelbarrow.
"I am going to work for the man
who builds houses," he said.
"I can not carry you."

"Then will you carry my pan of coconuts?
You can put them in the wheelbarrow."

Old Man began to laugh.
"Oh no, you lazy boy, I will not carry
your pan of coconuts,
but I know what to do.
I will sit in the wheelbarrow.
I will put the pan on my head.
You will push the wheelbarrow.
That is the way I will carry
your load."

Old Man did not wait for Gemo to say
Yes or No.
He sat down in the wheelbarrow and said,
"Put the pan on my head."

Now a small boy always does what
an old man tells him to do.
So Gemo put the pan of coconuts
on Old Man's head.

Gemo began to push the wheelbarrow.
It was very hard work.
He pushed and puffed,
    and he puffed and pushed.
The wheelbarrow moved slowly.

At last Gemo said, “Old Man,
this wheelbarrow gives me a hard time.
I will carry my pan of coconuts myself.”
And Gemo put the pan of coconuts
on his own head.

Old Man said, “Now you know
a good thing.
You know you can carry your own load.”

“Yes, Old Man,” Gemo said.
“Now I know that for true.”

Gemo walked fast.
He must get to market soon.
He must sell the coconuts today.
His load did not seem so heavy now.
He did not stop to ask anyone to carry him.
He let his own two feet carry him
all the way to the market.

When the coconuts were all sold
Gemo bought some fish.
He put the fish in the pan.
He put the pan on his head and went home.

All along the way the rice birds made
plenty, plenty palaver.
Talk, talk, talk, all the way home.
"Carry your own load," they said.
"Carry it, carry it, carry it your own self."

Gemo said, "Don't tell me that thing!
I know it.
Everybody knows he must carry his own load."
And he walked along fast, his head load
sitting well on his head.

Gemo felt very wise inside.
He had learned a big thing,
and he had learned it all by himself.
You just don't say to everyone,
"Will you carry me?"
You carry your own self.
That's for true!